SWITCH

Chameleon Chaos

Ali Sparkes

illustrated by

Ross Collins

OXFORD
UNIVERSITY PRESS

OXFORD
UNIVERSITY PRESS

Great Clarendon Street, Oxford OX2 6DP

Oxford University Press is a department of the University of Oxford.
It furthers the University's objective of excellence in research, scholarship,
and education by publishing worldwide in

Oxford   New York

Auckland   Cape Town   Dar es Salaam   Hong Kong   Karachi
Kuala Lumpur   Madrid   Melbourne   Mexico City   Nairobi
New Delhi   Shanghai   Taipei   Toronto

With offices in

Argentina   Austria   Brazil   Chile   Czech Republic   France   Greece
Guatemala   Hungary   Italy   Japan   Poland   Portugal   Singapore
South Korea   Switzerland   Thailand   Turkey   Ukraine   Vietnam

Oxford is a registered trade mark of Oxford University Press
in the UK and in certain other countries

British Library Cataloguing in Publication Data
Data available

ISBN: 978-0-19-913735-0
1 3 5 7 9 10 8 6 4 2

Printed in Great Britain

Paper used in the production of this book is a natural,
recyclable product made from wood grown in sustainable forests.
The manufacturing process conforms to the environmental
regulations of the country of origin.

Photograph on page 127: Thanks to Tiny Drury, cool chameleon.

Josh

- **FULL NAME:** Josh Phillips
- **AGE:** 8 years
- **HEIGHT:** Taller than Danny
- **FAVOURITE THING:** Collecting insects
- **WORST THING:** Skateboarding
- **AMBITION:** To be an entomologist

Petty

- **FULL NAME:** Petty Hortense Potts
- **AGE:** None of your business
- **HEIGHT:** Head and shoulders above every other scientist
- **FAVOURITE THING:** SWITCHing Josh & Danny
- **WORST THING:** Evil ex-friend Victor Crouch
- **AMBITION:** Adoration and recognition as the world's most genius scientist (and for the government to say sorry!)

CONTENTS

Framed

As he hung by his feet from the bars, Josh reflected that this was not a good day.

His school shoes were laced firmly to the bridge of the climbing frame. The laces would probably snap if he relaxed his feet out of their rigid hook-shape and slid off the metal rung— but this could only lead to another problem. There was a metre of drop below him and it was a soft landing. A soft, *muddy* landing.

A week of rain had turned the whole playground into a swamp. The caretaker had even put cones and orange tape up around the climbing frame to stop anyone getting onto it. When Josh finally staggered into class like a mud monster the teachers would be in no doubt that he'd broken the rules and gone onto the climbing frame. He'd be in a lot of trouble, even though it wasn't his fault.

He had tried to swing himself up, grab the bars and get an arm through one so he could untie his feet with his spare hand—but he couldn't manage it. He just wasn't good at being upside down—and the longer he hung here the more his head threatened to explode. He felt as if his eyeballs were getting bigger with every passing minute.

No. On balance, this was not a good day. Josh really needed some help. He really needed Danny, his twin brother. But as everyone had now gone back into class, it didn't look as though anyone would be coming by soon.

His feet were beginning to shake horribly now, with the effort of staying sharply bent like right-angled hooks. Josh called 'Help!' a few times. Nobody came. It really looked as if he was going to end the afternoon looking like a hippo.

He wrapped his arms around his head and bunched up his eyes. He was going to have to drop and snap the laces. His feet just couldn't stay like this . . .

'Josh? What on earth are you doing, you peculiar child?'

'Gah!' grunted Josh. His eyes pinged open again and he saw the bristly upside-down chin of Petty Potts twenty centimetres from his face.

'Getmyleeegs!' he gurgled. 'Quiiick! I'm going to—gah!'

SLIP.
SNAP.
DOOF.

Josh found himself on the ground, gasping and gurgling as his blood-filled brain spun and his vision wavered. On the bright side, he seemed to have avoided the worst of the mud. He realized Petty Potts had grabbed him just as his laces snapped. This had converted his fall from a straight drop to a sudden slither. His trousers were a bit muddy but there were only a couple of splodges on his school shirt.

Petty crouched down, peering at him through her thick-lensed spectacles, and scratched her wiry thatch of grey hair. 'Are you in training for the Olympics?' she enquired.

'No!' huffed Josh, carefully getting up on to his elbows. His head swooshed about as the blood in it started to get back to other locations in his body. 'Not unless there's a medal for getting stupidly in the way of even stupider school bullies. I'd probably get gold for that!'

'Oh dear,' Petty said, helping him to his feet. 'Who was it?'

Josh shook his head and screwed up his eyes again.

14

'Well, you don't have to worry about snitching to me, do you?' Petty said. 'I'm not your teacher. I'm just your kindly next-door neighbour.'

'Kindly?' spluttered Josh. He could think of a lot of words which would describe Petty Potts— grumpy, eccentric, genius, amazing, barmy, and dangerous were the first ones that came to mind. But she *had* just saved him from a bath of sticky brown goo and a severe telling off back in class.

He sighed. 'Billy Sutter and Jason Bilk,' he muttered.

'Aaaah,' Petty said, as if she had a clue who he was talking about.

'They were just about to commit mass anticide,' Josh explained. 'They were heading for my ant farm that I set up for the class—with a bottle of boiling hot water! They were going to boil two hundred and fifty-four defenceless ants alive! I had to throw my lunch at them to stop them.'

'Aaaah,' Petty said again, but more sympathetically this time. She knew that Josh was nuts about creepy-crawlies—and all kinds of wildlife. She also knew that he would feel extra sensitive about protecting the ants, because not that long ago, she'd turned him into one. 'And for this act of mercy you were tied upside down to the climbing frame.'

'Only after the swirly,' Josh sighed. His short blond hair was still a bit wet from the flushing and smelt of toilet cleaner. 'And the wedgy.' He tugged self-consciously at his trousers and felt the material give a bit.

'Want me to SWITCH them into ants so you can stamp on them?' Petty offered.

Josh looked at her, his head on one side and his eyes narrowed. It was a good thing she didn't know who Billy Sutter and Jason Bilk were because he wouldn't put it past her to SWITCH them. Petty might look like a nice old lady but she was actually a brilliant scientist with a secret underground laboratory beneath her garden shed, where she worked on her SWITCH project. Over the summer, since he and Danny had first stumbled upon her secret, Petty had recruited them to help her— whether they liked it or not. Back then they knew nothing about Petty's SWITCH sprays.

Her BUGSWITCH spray could hijack your cells and turn you into an insect or spider. And her AMPHISWITCH spray could turn you into an amphibian. And, after he and Danny had helped her find the lost formula to REPTOSWITCH, Petty now had a SWITCH spray to turn them into reptiles too.

'Well?' Petty was prodding his shoulder. 'Shall I SWITCH them into ants? I might even have that spray on me . . . ' And she started patting the pockets of her big, slightly grubby overcoat.

'No, Petty! Don't even think about it!' warned Josh. 'And what are you doing here anyway? Why are you at our school?' He felt very uneasy. Petty had a habit of showing up in their everyday lives . . . and it usually led to some kind of SWITCH-related danger.

'I was just passing when I saw you, that's all,' Petty said. 'I came in at the gate (your school security is *so* lax) and popped along to find out what you were up to. Would you rather I hadn't? Would you like to be back up on the bars?'

'Sorry—no,' Josh mumbled. 'And thanks . . . really. But . . . oh heck—I've got to get back into class. I'll be in such trouble!'

'Run along then, run along,' chirruped Petty. 'And bring Danny with you to see me after school. I think it's time we went to C Phase of REPTOSWITCH.'

'C Phase?' Josh called back as he began to run towards the low red-brick building. He felt a lurch of excitement. He and Danny had been lizards already and although—once again—they'd nearly got themselves eaten, it had still been amazing. He couldn't wait to have another go. They would be more careful with C Phase . . . whatever it was.

Petty tapped her nose and winked elaborately. 'C Phase!' she called after him. 'Find out after school!'

'Josh! Where on earth have you been?' demanded Miss Mellor as soon as he got into the classroom. Twenty-seven pairs of eyes swivelled onto him. They included Danny's, who was making a 'What the heck?!!' face—and Billy Sutter's and Jason Bilk's, who were making 'Tell and your life is OVER' faces.

'Got stuck in the toilet,' Josh said. Several of the girls giggled.

'So I see,' Miss Mellor said. 'Maybe next time, before you come back to class, you might think about pulling your trousers up first.'

Josh stared down at his legs and saw, to his horror, that his energetic tug to undo Billy and Jason's gift of a wedgy had gone too far. A button on his trousers had pinged off and the panicked running down the corridor had made the zip give way and now, even as his eyes bulged in disbelief, his muddy grey trousers were sliding down to his knees.

Josh felt himself go scarlet all over as the whole class collapsed into shrieks of laughter and catcalls. Danny buried his face in his hands and even Miss Mellor was pressing her mouth shut tight, trying to look as if she wasn't rupturing herself laughing too.

Josh groaned as he hitched his trousers up, and wished he could just blend into the wall and disappear.

C Phase

'SUTTER! I'm gonna spread you like BUTTER!' Danny yelled. 'BILK I'm gonna spill you like MILK! You've just asked for DOUBLE TROUBLE.'

'Well . . . thanks, Danny,' Josh said. 'It's nice of you to threaten my enemies for me—in poem format. Like the dairy theme, too. It'd be even *more* impressive if they were *here.*'

Danny glanced around. The only scare he'd caused was to a passing cat, which shrank away from him on the top of a wall as they walked down their road after school. 'I'm just warming up,' he said. 'I will be telling them that tomorrow. You don't think I'd let them get away with giving you a swirly and a wedgy and then tying you upside-down to a climbing frame by your shoelaces, do you?'

Josh shuddered. All of that was pretty bad—but the trousers bit at the end had been worse. Billy Sutter and Jason Bilk had been crying with laughter—the whole class had. He had paid dearly for defending the ant colony. Very dearly.

'Thanks, Danny,' he mumbled. 'But the best thing we can do is forget it. I'll just keep my head down and do my best not to get noticed for a few days.'

'You're kidding! We've got to get revenge!' spluttered Danny and his spiky blond hair seemed to bristle with fury. 'It's a matter of honour!'

'Revenge,' sighed Josh. 'Danny—have you noticed the *size* of Billy Sutter and Jason Bilk this term? They're like escapees from one of your computer games! They've got fists like lump-hammers. And they nearly killed you in the summer term, remember? They nearly stamped you to death!'

'Yeah . . . true . . .' admitted Danny. 'But I was a grasshopper at the time.'

'That's not the point,' Josh said. 'They're mental and dangerous. We need to keep away from them.'

'Yoooo–hooo!' A familiar voiced trilled
out through the warm afternoon air. 'Jo–osh!
Danneee!'

Danny grinned at Josh. 'I know what will take
your mind off Sutter and Bilk,' he said, as Petty
Potts ambled down her front path towards them.

'Aaah yes.' Josh smiled. 'C Phase!'

Petty led them down the side passage into her
back garden, which was possibly more overgrown
than they'd ever seen it. Over the summer it had
filled with weeds, which had grown so high they
now had to pick their way through a roughly
beaten tunnel which Petty had made.

'Don't you ever get out your lawnmower?' asked Josh as he got hit in the face by a lively thistle.

'What on earth for?' called back Petty. 'I don't want any spies being able to see into my garden and my shed. And anyway, Josh, I would have thought you'd approve—my garden is a perfect haven for wildlife.'

This was confirmed by a shriek from Danny as a cricket jumped out of the unruly thicket onto his shoulder. 'GETITOFFMEEEE,' he yelped and Josh automatically turned and collected the minibeast from him. He was well used to Danny's heebie-jeebies about creepy-crawlies. It didn't seem to matter how often Danny had been SWITCHed into a creepy-crawly himself, they still freaked him out.

'It's a beauty,' Josh murmured, peering into his cupped hands at the big, bright-green cricket. 'A Great Green Bush Cricket. They love this kind of tall weedy garden. Look at those legs! Remember how brilliant it felt when we had legs like that?' He let the creature jump back into the weeds, gazing after it with fascination. 'You know, when we were grasshoppers that time . . . ?'

Danny was still shuddering and checking his shoulders for other insects when they arrived at the shed door behind Petty. 'Forget insects!' He grinned as Petty walked through the very ordinary looking shed and pulled a bit of old sheet at the far wall to one side. 'We're up to reptiles now!'

Petty turned and smiled at them, one grey eyebrow raised behind her smeary spectacles, and pushed open the secret door behind the sheet. On the other side of it was a set of steps leading down into a passageway with curved corrugated iron overhead. It had once been a wartime bomb shelter . . . but now it was a passage to something far more extraordinary—Petty's secret underground laboratory.

They followed her much more eagerly than they might have done a few weeks ago. Petty had a habit of tricking them into helping with her research—a habit which had nearly got them killed more times now than they could count. But now that they'd discovered the REPTOSWITCH formula and had moved up the food chain a bit, the idea of being SWITCHed had become more exciting than scary.

The laboratory was filled with peculiar things. Various sinister looking liquids in bottles stood on the long workbench and along shelves were books and bottles and a cage of mice. Odd gadgets were lying around and a computer glowed in a small booth in one corner. In the middle of the room was a rectangular see–through plastic tent—the main SWITCHing zone where Petty could spray her subjects (usually Josh and Danny) but keep out of the spray herself.

'You haven't started packing everything up yet, then?' Danny said.

'I beg your pardon?' replied Petty, going into her booth and punching some of the keys on the computer.

'You said you were going to move away because you were being spied on, remember?' Danny said. 'After you turned us into lizards—after your kitchen window got broken.'

'I am quite aware of what I said,' snapped Petty.

'And I meant it . . . at the time. But everything's been nice and quiet since, so although I am still planning a new, much more secret laboratory, I'm not moving house *just* yet. That—after all—is exactly what they'll *expect* me to do!'

'Who?' Josh asked. 'Who will expect you to?'

'Well—the spies, of course!' Petty said, with an exasperated tone. 'I've told you—I'm always being watched!'

Josh and Danny exchanged looks. A couple of weeks ago they would have rolled their eyes at each other but on the day that Petty's window had been broken it turned out that somebody *was* watching. Only . . . they were watching *Josh and Danny*. And sending them messages . . . clues . . . in marbles!

'Shall we tell her?' muttered Danny.

Josh shook his head. 'Not now. Not until after this SWITCH. We don't want her going all weird again like she did last time.'

'Now—do you want to go on with this silly conversation or do you want to go to C Phase?' Petty asked, emerging from her computer booth with a spray bottle in one hand and a wild look in her eyes. The light from her old PC monitor shone green across one side of her face. She looked like an evil genius on the verge of a dastardly master plan. Then she stoutly broke wind and muttered ''Scuse me!' It sort of spoilt the effect.

'What's C Phase?' Danny asked, waving his hand rapidly in front of his face. 'Crocodile Phase? Is it? Is it crocodile SWITCH?'

'No, Danny—not yet,' Petty said. 'I told you—we need to build up slowly. You were lizards last time, which seemed to be quite successful—now it's time to move up to . . . CHAMELEON!'

There was a pause.

'Chameleon?' echoed Danny. 'Chameleon?' He looked deeply unimpressed.

Josh was looking much more excited. 'Wow! Chameleon! They're . . . amazing! Weird! Brilliant!'

'What? They never blummin' move!' squawked

Danny. 'I've seen them in pet shops. They just sit there on a stick with their eyes going all googly.'

'I don't care,' Josh said. 'I still want to be one! They're Little Lions—didn't you know? That's what chameleon means. Or "Earth Lion" because some of them have those sort of mane shaped things round their heads. They're amazing—like dragons.'

'Well, I was like a dragon when I was a sand lizard,' grumped Danny. 'But I could run about and climb trees like lightning. A chameleon would take about a week to get up my leg.'

'Well don't bother then,' Josh said. 'I'll do it!'

So Danny stood back and watched as Josh went into the spraying tent. But then he huffed and said he might as well, seeing as Josh was going to, although this was going to be really boring. And he followed his brother in.

'Right—here we go,' Petty said, retreating through the plastic sheeting and holding out the spray in one hand. A second later a fine bluish mist fell across Josh and Danny and they stood very still, and waited . . .

Surprise!!!

And waited. And waited a bit longer.

'Oh dear,' Petty said after a full minute had passed. 'Maybe I've sprayed you with something else . . . '

'That's not a sentence you ever want to hear from an unstable genius,' muttered Danny, feeling distinctly edgy.

Petty was examining the spray and now she was taking it across to her lab bench, putting a drop of it carefully onto a glass slide and peering at it through her microscope. She checked her formula back in the computer booth and then came out to peer at the slide again. 'No—it's definitely correct,' she said. 'Although this Serum Which Instigates Total Cellular Hijack doesn't seem to be instigating anything at all this time.'

Josh and Danny, still unchanged, shrugged at her through the plastic.

'Perhaps, as chameleons move so slowly,' pondered Petty, 'the whole process of cellular hijack is slow too . . . although the mice SWITCHed soon enough . . . '

Danny and Josh waited for half an hour and in the end they went home for tea.

'It's most upsetting,' Petty said as they headed back out through the shed. 'And most disappointing. But I suppose even a genius like me can't expect perfect results every time. Come back tomorrow and we'll try again . . . '

'Maybe she's losing her touch,' Josh said as they arrived back in their own front garden.

'Or her mind,' added Danny.

'Look,' Josh said, casting a glance around the garden. 'She's not the only one who thinks she's being watched these days, is she? I mean . . . since the marble thing started . . . '

Danny didn't answer for a while. He sat down on the sun-warmed red tiles of their doorstep and Josh sat next to him. 'I know what you mean,' he said. 'But it's been two weeks now since we found the marble with the code in. And whoever sent us the first marble and the clues hasn't been back in touch again. So maybe it *was* just someone having a silly joke and that's that.'

Josh looked at him. He knew Danny didn't really believe that. The marble thing was weird. The first marble they'd been sent had been an ordinary one —but the next one they'd found, after following the clue, had code in it. It was like the code in the glass cubes which made up Petty's BUGSWITCH and REPTOSWITCH formulae. But whoever had sent them to find the marble—it wasn't Petty.

'Let's tell Petty about the marble tomorrow, after school,' Josh said. 'She's calmed down a bit since the broken window thing. So she probably won't freak out too much if we tell her now.'

Suddenly the front door opened and Mum was there, staring down at them, smiling. 'There you are!' she exclaimed. 'I've been wondering where you'd got to. I've got a surprise for you! It looks like you've won something.'

Josh and Danny followed her into the hallway,

curious to see what she meant. Piddle, their dog (named after a habit he had when he got over-excited) danced around their feet as if he was fascinated by the post too. Mum picked up a small cardboard package with both of their names, their address, and a big sticker on it which read 'CONGRATULATIONS! COMPETITION WINNERS!'

'Go on then!' urged Mum. 'Open it!'

'Must be one of Josh's wildlife competition things,' Danny said. 'Nice of you to enter both of us.'

It seemed Danny was right. Josh often went in for competitions in his wildlife magazines. The prize was a shiny box set of six small books about wildlife—all kinds of animals from panthers and lions to bats and rats. There was a brief note with the prize but it didn't tell them much. It just said, in printed letters, 'Well done! You're the winner of the Chatz TV channel Marbellous Mammals competition!' There was a website address but no phone number or any further information.

'Well, that's nice! From Chatz TV too! That's

the channel Jenny and I watch—the Darcy
Show and all that. I didn't know you'd entered a
competition with Chatz TV, Josh!'

'Nor did I,' Josh said.

'Well—well done! You can share those, can't
you?' Mum said, giving their hair a ruffle and then
wandering off upstairs.

Danny nodded and said, 'Yeah—they're cool
books. Well done, Josh.'

But Josh wasn't saying anything. He was staring
at the note and looking odd. Then he was staring
at the box set of books and looking . . . odder.
When Mum had gone all the way upstairs he
glanced up at Danny and said, 'Back garden—
bush den—now!'

Danny ran after his brother, puzzled. Piddle
followed them, his tongue hanging out. Once
inside the woody den beneath the rhododendron
bush Josh sat cross-legged on the earthy floor
and flipped the note around for Danny to read.
As Piddle skidded in beside them Danny read it
quickly. 'Yeah? What?' he said.

Josh huffed in frustration. 'Didn't you see it? LOOK! Read it properly!'

'I did,' argued Danny. 'It says "Well done! You're the winner of the Marvellous Mammals competition!" So what?'

'Not marvellous,' Josh said, looking a little wild-eyed himself. 'MarBellous.'

'What?' Danny said. 'A spelling mistake?'

Josh biffed him on the head with the box set. 'As in MARBLE, you dipstick!'

Danny went quiet and rubbed Piddle's floppy ears thoughtfully. 'You think it's from the Mystery Marble Sender?'

'I'm certain of it,' Josh said, tipping the six books out into his lap and sticking his fingers into the empty box. He sucked in a quick breath . . . 'Because of this.'

And he held up another note—with the same strange spiky handwriting as before. At the top it read:

HELLO AGAIN, JOSH + DANNY. ARE YOU READY FOR ANOTHER CLUE . . . ?

Slow Pokes

WITH EACH YOU FIND,
YOU MOVE CLOSER TO YOUR DESTINY.
DARE YOU SEEK?

Danny stared at the note in Josh's hands.
'That's what the first one said, isn't it?' he whispered
and Josh nodded. Below was another clue—
presumably leading them to another coded marble.
It read:

CLUE 2: GO WHERE MANY FEET ARE BARE.
RISE TO THE LIGHT. SLIP AND YOU WILL BURN.

Josh looked at Danny. Danny looked at Josh.
'Any ideas?' he asked.
Josh shrugged. 'Nope. Doesn't make much
sense, does it? "Go where many feet are bare?"
Where's that then?'
'The bathroom?' ventured Danny.

'But—many feet? I mean . . . there's only the
five of us—Mum, Dad, Jenny, and you and me—
who go to the bathroom with bare feet.'

'Well—that's ten feet . . . Let's look anyway,'
Danny said.

Two minutes later they stood in the bathroom,
looking around for a mysterious coded marble.
Piddle had lost interest by now and remained in
the garden, chasing his tail.

'Rise to the light. Slip and you will burn,' read
out Josh, still clutching the note. They peered at
the bathroom light. It was just an ordinary bulb
under an ordinary shade. It wasn't the kind of
shade that anything could be put into—it was just
a cone, hanging open.

'You could slip in a bathroom,' murmured
Danny. 'But why would you burn? There's nothing
hot here—except if you filled the bath right up and
. . . no. Then you'd boil! Or scald or something. It
doesn't make sense.'

Josh sighed and shrugged and put the note,
folded up, into his pocket. 'Let's sleep on it
tonight,' he said. 'See if the answer comes when

we wake up tomorrow.'

They were both late for school the next morning. Not because they were distracted by thinking about the clue—they'd more or less forgotten it when they woke up—but because time started messing with their heads. It started going really fast. And they, it seemed, were going really SLOW.

They took ages to get up and then a lifetime to wash. Then their porridge went cold and solid before they'd eaten even half of it. And with only five minutes to go before they had to leave for school, they were both still staring at their socks and nowhere near finding their shoes. Mum had asked them to put socks and shoes on about

 seven times before Dad got involved and told them off for winding everyone up.

The weird thing, though, thought Josh, was that he *wasn't* winding anyone up. He was doing everything normally—it was just that Mum and Dad seemed rather hyper and busy and fast today. Danny agreed as they walked to school. Last term Mum used to give them a lift as the school was about half an hour's walk away—but this term Dad had said they should walk. It was safe enough and the exercise was good for them.

And so they had been walking and it wasn't too bad and they usually made it in to class on time.

Not today. When Danny and Josh arrived, the playground was completely empty and the lollipop man was heading home with his STOP sign under his arm. Josh stared at his watch in disbelief. 'It's a quarter past nine!' he gasped. 'How did that happen?'

They got another telling off from Miss Mellor when they got in. She accused them of dawdling and messing about and having no respect for her time and the gift of education. And so on.

It was not a good day. Again, thought Josh. And it didn't get much better as the morning wore on. When everyone else handed in their maths tests Danny was only on question three out of ten. And Josh was only on question four. Miss Mellor sniffed with disapproval when she collected them from their desks and glared at them both. 'Is this some kind of a joke? Or a dare?' she asked, scrutinizing first Josh and then Danny.

They just stared up at her, open mouthed and confused, and then Danny's left eyeball rolled so far round into his eye socket that Miss Mellor went pale and had to sit down on Claudia Petherwaite's desk in shock. She sent him to see the receptionist who doubled as a school nurse.

'That was freaky,' Danny mumbled to himself as he ambled along the corridor. He did feel a little weird today. The eyeball thing was peculiar but odder still was the way that—right now—he really wanted to climb into the ornamental weeping fig tree next to the head teacher's office. No—really! He wanted it *so* much. Like he wanted to ride the rollercoaster at Chessington World of Adventure. Like he wanted a mountain bike with shock absorbers. That *tree*! That amaaaaazing tree!

It was a beautiful specimen—as tall as a man and bristling with happy, healthy green leaves. Its trunk and branches had been artfully encouraged to grow into attractive twists and gnarls. The head teacher was very proud of it—he'd brought it in from his own conservatory—but he certainly would never have expected one of his pupils to stand riveted before it, staring at his Ficus Benjamina as if it was the latest thrill ride at a theme park.

As Danny gazed at the tree in wonder, he realized his eyeball must wait. He *had* to get closer to those branches.

One second he was putting his school shoe carefully into the large earthenware pot where the tree was rooted in moist earth—and the next he was climbing up the trunk. With five green toes on each hand and foot. And two amazing rotating eyeballs. And a wide, lazy grin across his scaly face. Must tell Petty, he thought to himself as one pincer-like hand worked across the other, steadily pulling him up into the tree. I'm a chameleon at last! Her SWITCH spray *does* work . . .

Fig Role

'PE after break, everybody,' called out Miss Mellor as the bell went. 'Don't dawdle in the playground. Get back inside and get into your PE kit as soon as the bell goes again.'

Josh groaned. With everyone going so fast today there was no way he would be able to get out to the playground and get back in again and get his PE kit on in time. He just knew it. So he didn't go out. He slid slowly and quietly under his desk as everyone else went outside and Miss Mellor didn't notice as she gathered up some papers and her spectacle case and made for the staff room and a cup of tea. As soon as the door closed behind her Josh dug out his PE kit and ambled to the boys' changing rooms to get a head start. He hoped Danny's eyeball was OK. That was seriously weird.

He thought about going off to find his brother but he knew it would take too long. He guessed he should be more worried, really, but . . . he just couldn't work up the energy.

Danny had never felt so relaxed in his life. Normally he was scared after SWITCHing—or at least highly excited. But this time he was just . . . cool. True, it was a little bit chilly—he would like to be a bit warmer. And as he thought this he spotted something extremely useful on the wall just below the branch he was clinging to. It was a small cream–coloured box with a dial on it. A thermostat! It was the control for the heating in this corridor. Brilliant. Very slowly and steadily Danny extended his back leg and, closing the two toes on it like a scaly green pincer, he nudged the thermostat dial all the way round to the hottest end. The small grilled radiator below him began to waft up warmer air. Oooooooh—nice!

Then he climbed a little higher and discovered his own reflection, staring back at him from the glass of a framed certificate on the wall.

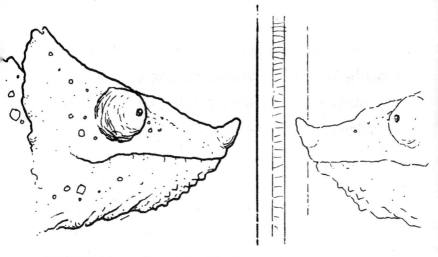

WOW! He really wished Josh was here to see
this. He looked amazing! I take it all back about
chameleons being boring, he thought. He was a
splendid creature. He was much chunkier than
last time, when he'd been a sand lizard. Then
he'd been slick and quick and now, although he
was slow, his looks more than made up for it. He
was the most beautiful emerald green all along his
finely-scaled sides, and his tail, which was long,
curled into a perfect coil underneath him, like an
unfurled bracken leaf. He had a magnificent crest
along his spine, rising like a decorative fan from
the back of his neck. There seemed to be rather
prehistoric looking bony plates across his forehead
and a sort of mini-crest down his nose, ending in

a small horn. A ridge of tiny spikes ran under his chin like an elegantly trimmed beard and he had a gently smiling mouth. Opening his jaws, Danny saw two neat rows of sharp teeth and a squishy pink tongue rolled up in the bottom of his mouth.

And his eyes were amazing—poking up out of his face like pointy green ping-pong balls. There was just a small dot of black in the centre of each of them and they could roll all over the place in their sockets. He could see right down his tail with one while checking out the small horn on his nose with the other. And it all seemed perfectly natural.

Danny sighed contentedly. This was definitely the most chilled-out SWITCH he'd ever had. Nothing was going to eat him or stamp on him. And he was up in this fantastic tree! He might just take a little nap . . .

And then a THUNDEROUS noise vibrated through his head, nearly knocking him off his branch.

Danny quickly realized what it was. The bell for break had just gone. Soon there was more noise—the rumble of 250 kids piling out of their classrooms and along the corridors, heading for the playground. They surged past him with an immense roar, filling his skull with brain-shaking thuds and rumbles. With a sudden skip in his easy-going heart, it occurred to Danny that he might be spotted here, in the tree. What if they could see him?

And as he thought this and his heart did a few more nervous skips, he realized that something was changing. It felt as if waves of warmth were washing over his scales. Checking out his sides with his gyrating eyes, he saw exactly what was going on. He was changing. He was getting a camouflage make-over, right now! His emerald green scales were now a softer green with little specks of darker green blooming into view across some brand-new wavy stripes of paler green. It was incredible! There were even some brown stripes coming out now. He was exactly the same colour as the twigs and leaves of the tree all around him. All he had to do was keep very, very still, and none of the kids would see him.

And that was very easy.

Soon the hubbub died away and Danny's head stopped vibrating with the noise. And as everything calmed down he was able to make out people actually talking. Two people. They were huddled together just beneath him, hiding behind the tree and talking in hissy voices.

'He got himself down yesterday. And he missed the mud!'

Danny recognized the voice—and the smell—of Billy Sutter. Next came the high pitched wheezy laugh of Jason Bilk as he agreed, 'Yeah! But his trousers fell down! That was well funny! Did you see his face? Like a strawberry!'

'We can have some more laughs with him in PE,' replied Billy. 'When Miss is timing the girls on the circuit training we can hang him upside down on the ropes!'

There was more tittering as Danny realized, with some concern, who they were talking about. Josh! Billy and Jason were going to get at his brother again. He felt anger rush across his scales and saw that his camouflage was holding, but flickering, and little spots of red were showing up here and there.

'But what if we get seen?' whispered Jason. 'The school will phone up my dad again and he'll go mental!'

'We won't get seen!' hissed Billy. 'And anyway, we'll make out he *asked* us to help him get up. He's much too wimpy to snitch on us. You wait— it's gonna be *so funny*! His little eyeballs are gonna pop! Puny little bug freak!'

Danny felt fury chasing his anger now. *He* was the only one entitled to call Josh a freak. Josh undoubtedly *was* a freak when it came to his love of creepy-crawlies, but Danny wasn't going to stand for having a dipstick like Billy Sutter or Jason Bilk get away with saying it!

Trouble was, by the time he'd got down to gore them with his nose horn, they'd long gone.

A Bit Ropey

Even with a fifteen minute head start, most of
the other boys arrived and got ready before Josh.
When they all piled into the changing room after
break and got their shoes, socks, and uniforms off
and their PE shorts and T–shirts on, Josh was still
slo—o—o—o—wly pulling his T–shirt over his
head.

There was no sign of Danny when he eventually
followed the others into the school hall, which
doubled as a gym. It had a rack of climbing bars
designed to be pulled out from one wall on wheels
and fixed firmly into the floor with bolts. A
vaulting box had been put out at one end of the
hall, along with hula hoops and beanbags. Josh
hoped his brother was OK—but he guessed he
was probably having a little doze on the 'sick kid

sofa' behind reception. Maybe they'd get Mum to come and collect him and take him home. Josh wished he'd done that mad eyeball thing too so they could *both* go. Trying to keep up with all these hyperactive kids was really taking it out of him! Hmmm . . . the mad eyeball made him think of something . . . what . . . ? Nah. Josh yawned. It was gone.

'OK—girls down this end!' called out Miss Mellor, pointing to the vaulting box and hoops and beanbags. 'And boys to the climbing frame and the ropes.' She got out her stopwatch and turned away to supervise the handing out of beanbags and hoops.

Josh sighed as all the boys rushed for the bars. Climbing the bars was quite fun. You could easily get up quite high and sit on them, swinging your legs about. But the four ropes which dangled along one stretch of the equipment were much harder. The thick twists of tight cord were heavy, weighed down with a knot at the bottom—and once you'd got your feet on the knot and reached up there was no more help. You just had to pull yourself up with your hands, knees, and feet. Josh was rubbish at the ropes. He felt as if his limbs were made of weak, bendy wire whenever he tried. Danny was great at it but Josh just wasn't.

And now that all the boys had beaten him to the bars there was no space left except on the ropes. The ropes were all he could do.

'Need a hand, bug freak?' said a voice in his ear and three seconds later, once again, he was upside down. There were hoots of laughter from other boys on the climbing bars as Billy Sutter and Jason Bilk grabbed him, flipped him over, and then wrapped one rope around each leg three times. Josh didn't even have time to shout as he hung there, his legs trapped in the ropes, his upended head swinging back and forth a metre above the gym mats.

He felt dizzy for a moment as Billy's face swung close and then far and then close again, gurning at him. 'Baby want a push?' he mocked and shoved Josh in the chest so he swung harder. 'Baby want another push?' Some of the other kids had noticed and were laughing at him. He felt his face turn beetroot red again.

Miss Mellor turned round and walked down to the boys' end of the hall, staring at her stopwatch. Billy and Jason suddenly leapt away from Josh and

ran towards the climbing bars with
innocent expressions on their faces.

Josh was now dangling on just
one rope. His left leg had shaken
free of the other one. But he wasn't
upside down any more. He was
climbing the rope. Slowly but very,
very surely. He had just become one
of the best climbers in the school
that day. He had also just become
about thirty centimetres long—
and grown a crest. And a horn
on his nose.

Miss Mellor didn't notice. She
just walked on towards the swinging
ropes and then started yelling up at
the boys on the bars to go up and
down in races rather than just dangle
there like lazy monkeys. None of
them seemed to have noticed Josh's
SWITCH either.

Up on his rope, climbing steadily
higher, Josh thought it was a shame

that he wasn't going to get any house points for his brilliant achievement that day. But he realized this wasn't Miss Mellor's fault. She didn't have great eyesight anyway and he was not only a fraction of the size he'd been five minutes ago— he was also beautifully camouflaged against the rope.

SO! Petty's chameleon SWITCH spray *did* work! Josh thought to himself. He looked at the pincer-like hand in front of him as it clenched the twisted cord of the rope and pulled him up. It was scaly and brilliantly efficient at grasping handholds. His arms were very strong and had no difficulty in hoisting his body weight higher, supported by equally strong and agile legs and a fabulous tail which wrapped around the rope and steadied him as he climbed. He was currently pale brown in colour, but he knew this was only because he had SWITCHed while on the rope. With his amazing 360 degree eyeballs he could watch the rope above him and see the boys over on the bar, racing up and down it as Miss Mellor timed them. Two of the boys were looking a bit confused though—and worried. Billy and Jason kept glancing up and then around the room—then looking at each other with expressions which clearly said, 'Where has the bug freak gone?'

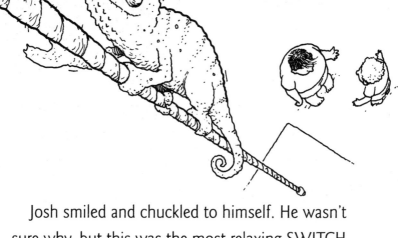

Josh smiled and chuckled to himself. He wasn't sure why, but this was the most relaxing SWITCH he'd ever had. He was really enjoying the feeling of strength that flowed through his reptilian muscles. I'm a Meller's chameleon! he realized, recognizing the horn on his nose and the crest along his spine. I can grow up to sixty centimetres and I can change colour and I can catch prey with my tongue! Woo–hoo! and . . . I can climb! I can *really* climb. Chameleons are tree dwellers—

they hardly ever come down to the ground! He just wished Danny was here to share all this information with him—even though he would almost certainly call him a nature nerd.

Hmmm—Danny. Josh paused in his climbing and his eyeballs rolled in all directions, taking in the whole school hall. No sign of his twin. He guessed that Danny might also have SWITCHed by now. He could be anywhere. Maybe the receptionist was screaming or phoning for the RSPCA to come and collect his brother right now.

Josh carried on climbing. It seemed like the best thing to do. He was so high now he could see the ceiling tiles in great detail. I've never climbed this high up before! he marvelled to himself. I always tried to . . . but I always ended up sliding down. He remembered the last time he'd really tried to get up the ropes. He'd made it as far as halfway, thanks to a boost from Danny when Miss Mellor wasn't looking—and then he'd just slid down and ended up with nasty rope burns on his arms and palms and the soles of his bare feet. Mum had put antiseptic cream on them when he got home.

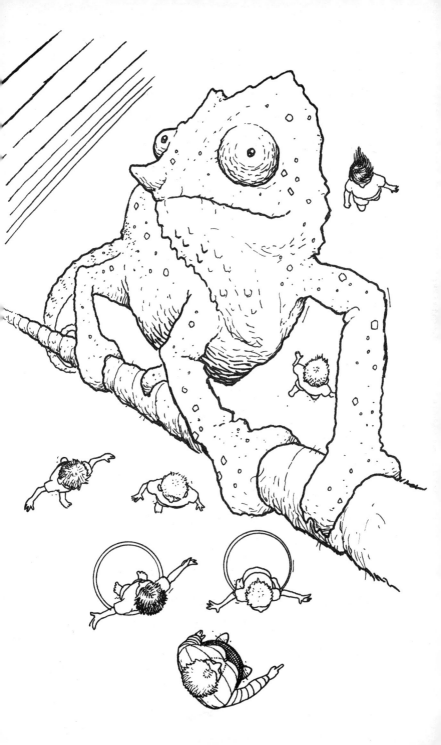

Josh suddenly froze on the rope, just as it connected to the long metal rung. Wait a minute! Bare feet . . . burning . . . why was that familiar? In a flash, the clue from the Mystery Marble Sender was in his head.

CLUE 2: GO WHERE MANY FEET ARE BARE. RISE TO THE LIGHT. SLIP AND YOU WILL BURN.

Many bare feet! There were at least twenty-six pairs of bare feet running around this hall now! And if you slipped on the rope (if you weren't a chameleon, of course) you would get rope burns! And . . . rise to the light? He tilted back his horned nose and rolled his eyeballs towards the ceiling. He was rising all right. *And* there were lights up here. Six of them!

He felt a surge of excitement in his scales as much as in his heart. They seemed to ripple and go a little pink. The hall light shades were square and flat, like shallow boxes made of white glass, hanging from metal struts. Once a year the caretaker got up on a special ladder to empty out all the dead moths and flies which collected in them. You could easily hide a marble in one.

Josh climbed onto the thick metal bar and made his way along to the far end of the frame. The nearest light was quite close by. He could almost reach across . . . Below him the PE lesson went on. The thuds and shouts and Miss Mellor's shrill whistle made his head vibrate a little, but he wasn't really aware of this—his eyes were fixed on the white glass shade. Chameleons have very good eyesight for reptiles, he remembered, hunting with stealth, using their excellent telescopic eyes. And now he used his excellent telescopic eyes on the light shade. He could climb across to it—but it might be dangerous. At least it wasn't hot. The day was bright and none of the lights were on. And now, tantalizingly, he could see something. Something round and shiny with a little blade of red rippling through it. It *was* the marble! He could see it clearly in the middle of the shade.

Suddenly he realized he didn't need to climb across. Josh lost no time—he opened his jaws and flung out an incredibly long, squishy, sticky tongue. It hurtled across into the light shade and stuck itself onto the marble—but as he snagged it back towards him the marble caught on a bit of electrical flex which wound into the shade. It pinged away across the shallow glass box and, to his enormous frustration, just out of reach. He tried again, hurling his tongue as far as it would go—but he couldn't reach. His amazingly long tongue was about half of his body length—but not long enough.

Josh couldn't bear to leave the marble up here. He was so close! He wrapped the end of his tail around the very edge of the frame and then tightly grasped the right-angled post with his back legs, while reaching out with his front legs (or arms). His strong hands gripped the edge of the shade and it didn't swing—it was held firmly by the metal strut. Using his tail to push his body across, Josh got himself safely on to the light shade. The marble lay in the far corner in a drift of dried-up insect body parts.

A second later, with a heavy clunk, the glass sphere was in his mouth, stuck to his tongue. A couple of dried-up bluebottle heads were in there too. Josh wasn't worried. For a chameleon, dried-up bluebottle heads were like dry roast peanuts. If he'd been in boy form that would probably have freaked him out, though.

A moment later Josh was in boy form.
And he was very freaked out.

Come on, Come on, Come on, Come on, Come on, Chameleon . . .

Petty Potts stood in her lab, holding one small black and white mouse in her palm and staring at it crossly.

'Come on, Hector! Look lively!' she chided. Hector stared back at her through beady black eyes. His whiskers twitched. He began to wash.

'You're supposed to be a chameleon by now!' Petty complained. 'The SWITCH formula is correct. You SWITCHed yesterday! Although . . . now that I come to think about it, I did get called away to answer the phone when I first sprayed you . . . so I actually didn't see precisely when you SWITCHed.' She pursed her lips and calculated. 'It could have been anything up to twenty minutes by the time I got off the phone and came back to look . . . Hector! Pay attention!' Hector stopped washing and looked at Petty, his furry head on one side. He seemed unimpressed.

'How long did it take you to SWITCH?' queried Petty, talking so close to the mouse that her breath made its poppy petal ears flicker. 'Of course—you're tiny and your heart beats around five hundred times a minute compared to a human heart of around seventy beats per minute . . . so if it *did* take you twenty minutes to SWITCH how long would it take Josh and Danny?'

Petty put Hector on her shoulder and grabbed a pencil and paper. It was time for some calculation. Hector burrowed happily into Petty's hair at the back of her neck while she did her working out. 'Don't poo down my collar!' she requested, scribbling at top speed. 'Now—height and weight plus metabolic rate . . . Hmmm,' she concluded. 'If my calculations are correct—and being as I'm a genius, they must be—then Josh and Danny may be having quite an interesting time at school today. Oh dear.'

Hector ambled slowly out onto Petty's other shoulder. He was bright green and not as surprised looking as he might have been. He was getting used to this SWITCHing lark.

'Ah—good—you SWITCHed!' Petty said, scooping the small chameleon into her hands.

'Erm . . . not *so* good,' added Petty a minute later. Something very peculiar had just happened. Something very peculiar indeed . . .

Head Start

Danny liked his head teacher. Mr Hurford was
a friendly man with a good sense of humour
and often ready for a joke while passing in the
corridor. He was also a strict man and nobody ever
messed around when he was running assembly or
stepping into their class for a while. Kids respected
him. Danny respected him. And liked him.

Although possibly not enough to throw himself
bodily around Mr Hurford's neck and cling on to
him.

Which is why it was really quite embarrassing
when this happened at 11.05a.m. that day, just
outside the head teacher's office.

The trouble was, Danny had just got a little too
relaxed. After failing to gore Billy Sutter and Jason
Bilk with his nose horn, Danny thought about

chasing after them as they walked away up the corridor. Then he thought better of it. There really was no way he was travelling anywhere faster than a dawdling snail right now. And even if he did catch up, Billy would have to stand patiently, waiting for him to expertly scale his leg, stomach and chest before Danny could attempt to very slowly gore his face.

Danny sighed and climbed back up the fig tree. As he made his careful way from branch to branch, snacking on a couple of small flies his tongue had found along the way, the bell went off again. It made his head buzz but at least he knew what it was this time and he was ready for the hubbub of all the kids coming back in from play and getting off to lessons. Within five minutes he was back on his favourite perch just above the radiator and as the heated air rose from it, gently warming his cold reptilian blood, Danny relaxed. He became perfectly still. Stiller than he had ever been. Even his heartbeat seemed to slow down. Before long, Danny nodded off.

The next thing he knew, someone was standing very close by and making hurrumphing noises. It took a moment, as his eyes rotated and focused on the sandy–haired head just below his branch, to work out who it was. Then Danny heard the hurrumpher say, 'Who the devil has been playing around with the thermostat? Hurrumph! My poor Ficus Benjamina will drop all its leaves in this heat!'

It was the head teacher! What if he looked up and saw him? Danny felt his scales pulse again and noticed darker flashes rolling across his camouflage.

He couldn't imagine what he would do if Mr Hurford discovered him.

Three seconds later Danny had no need to imagine. Mr Hurford discovered him. Not by peering up into the tree and gasping in amazement at the sight of a rather beautiful Meller's chameleon—but with a sudden DOOF! as Danny abruptly SWITCHed back to boy shape and fell onto his head.

'Gah—da—gah—wha? Wha? Gah? Wha?'

queried Mr Hurford as a healthy eight–year–old suddenly arrived out of thin air, whacked into his skull and slid down his back.

Danny was making similar noises of surprise and instinctively grabbing at the head teacher's neck to stop himself falling.

'What the blazes are you DOING?' squawked Mr Hurford as a Year Four boy finally tumbled onto the carpet. 'Danny? Is that you? Or . . . Josh? No . . . it has to be Danny!'

Danny had to think fast. What possible explanation could he offer for this situation? There wasn't an obvious bluff for this. *Falling Onto A Head Teacher (a guide)* was one self–help paperback he'd never seen at the local bookshop.

'I—I'm sorry. I—I was the one who turned up the heating,' spluttered Danny. 'I just wanted to confess . . . to throw myself . . . on your mercy,' he added.

The head teacher was straightening his tie and looking rather pink in the face. 'Danny—have you been watching *High School Musical* again? The entire box set, by any chance?' he queried.

'Errrm,' Danny said.

'Try to remember that we're not American teen idols,' sighed Mr Hurford. 'You don't need to hug me to avoid detention, you peculiar boy. Shouldn't you be in class, somewhere?'

'Yes—yes, I should,' muttered Danny, leaping to his feet. He was relieved to find that the 'being very slow' business seemed to have worn off.

'Run along then,' Mr Hurford said. 'And if you touch my thermostat again I'll have you shot,' he added, mildly.

Danny skidded into the school hall with his heart clattering. That was one very weird moment he'd just had there. Possibly the weirdest yet, since getting involved with Petty Potts and the SWITCH project (and that included being inside a cat's ear when he was a grasshopper several weeks back).

'Danny! Are you back with us?' called out Miss Mellor, pausing with her stopwatch in her hand. She seemed to have been timing a race up and down the climbing bars. 'Is your eye all right now?'

'Yes—yes, fine,' Danny said. 'Where's Josh?'

Miss Mellor looked around. 'I don't know. Has anyone seen Josh?' she called out to the class. Everyone looked around, murmuring, except, Danny noticed, Billy Sutter and Jason Bilk, who just looked at each other.

'Miss! Miss!' squeaked Claudia Petherwaite. 'He's up there!'

Everyone turned round and saw Josh.

He was hanging from the ceiling.

Boy-eleon

'I think one arm is longer than the other,' Josh
said, screwing up his face as he lifted his arms
and compared them. 'Or maybe it's just out of its
socket.'

'It's not,' Danny said. 'And you should be glad
they're not both broken. And your legs. And your
face. What were you thinking of, climbing into the
light shade? Are you nuts?'

The spectacle of Josh Phillips dangling from
the light had caused quite an uproar. Miss Mellor
screamed and Danny had shinned up the rope
at high speed. He hauled himself along the top
bar where Josh had been just minutes before in
chameleon form. As a crowd of kids and Miss
Mellor held their breath, Danny had anchored one
arm and one leg around the furthest corner of the

frame and then reached out and grabbed Josh's
flailing free hand.

At that moment the light shade had snapped
off its fixing and Josh dropped. But Danny had
got a good grip on him and his brother only fell
halfway, the shade smashing dramatically onto the
tumble mat below and making several girls (and
one or two boys) scream. Josh wrapped his legs
around the climbing frame post and gradually slid
to the floor amid a round of applause and whoops.

'What made you do it?' went on Danny as they
went out of the school gates and headed
for home.

'It seemed like a good idea at the time.'
Josh grinned. 'And it was really easy—I was a
chameleon, you see.'

'You too?' breathed Danny, turning to stare at
his twin. 'So was I! I was up in the fig tree in the
corridor! But nobody saw me—well, not until I fell
on Mr Hurford.' He went a little pink.

'You fell on Mr Hurford?' repeated Josh.

'Another time,' Danny said, waving his hand.
'Did anyone see you when you SWITCHed?'

'No!' Josh said, shaking his head. 'Nobody! I
was camouflaged to match the rope. I was halfway
up it anyway . . . well, thanks to Billy and Jason
putting me there, upside down!'

'I knew it! I heard them plotting when I was
up the tree. But I was too slow to do anything to
help,' shrugged Danny. 'Sorry!'

'No—no need!' grinned Josh. 'They did us a
favour! Remember the clue for the next marble?'

Danny wrinkled his brow, trying to remember.

'Go where many feet are bare. Rise to the light.
Slip and you will burn,' recited Josh. 'I was halfway up when I remembered. There were kids with

bare feet all over the place—and I've burnt myself on that rope before. Then I looked up and there was the light and in the light . . .' He pulled the marble out of his pocket and held it up in front of Danny's face '. . . was the marble!'

'Wow! Clever thinking for a nature nerd!' marvelled Danny.

'Shall we tell Petty about the marbles now, then?' Josh said. 'When we go back in to tell her about the SWITCH today?'

'Tell me *what*?'

Josh and Danny jumped as Petty suddenly loomed up between them. She was puffing as if she'd been running.

'Erm . . . ' Josh looked around them. They'd wandered along the edge of the woods which ran behind the school. There were other kids around but nobody close by. 'That we ended up SWITCHing today, in school,' he said.

'Oh dear! I feared as much,' Petty said. 'And worse . . .'

'What do you mean, worse?' asked Danny, looking nervous.

'Oh—oh nothing to really worry about,' Petty said in her special kind of light and airy voice. The kind which made Josh and Danny want to dive for cover and phone for Fire & Rescue.

'Wha—at?' Josh said, standing still and peering into Petty's eyes through her dusty spectacles.

'Well,' she said. 'I ran some tests on the REPTOSWITCH formula for chameleon. At first it seemed fine. Hector, my best mouse, did eventually SWITCH, like you did. It was a delayed reaction and I now know that the same thing happened yesterday. Then he SWITCHed back . . .'

'OK—he SWITCHed back—like we just did,' Danny said. 'And . . . ?'

'Well, when I say he SWITCHed back,' went on Petty, digging in the inside pocket of her crumpled old mac, 'I mean he SWITCHed back . . . mostly.'

Mostly? Josh and Danny looked at each other. They checked their legs and arms—everything seemed normal. It had happened once before with AMPHISWITCH. They'd been stuck with frog's legs for a couple of days after SWITCHing back, but there'd been an antidote.

'And then totally,' Petty continued. 'And then
. . . inexplicably . . . right back to mostly.' She
pulled something from her pocket. It was a mouse.
Mostly. Its little furry body and tail and legs were
definitely mouse . . . but on its shoulders was a
chameleon head. Hector looked quite cheesed off.
'He's a mouse–eleon!' sighed Petty. 'I have created
a small monster.'

It was a very odd moment. But it was broken
by two boys running past and shoving Josh into
Danny as they went.

'Seeyalater, bug freak and loser!' jeered Billy
and Jason. 'Have fun with your granny!'

A surge of annoyance went through Josh as
their enemies disappeared into the corner shop
to buy sweets. Maybe that's what did it—because
a second later there was a scaly green horn on
his nose.

'Uh–oh,' Petty said and swiftly propelled him behind a tree, out of sight. Danny ran after them and by the time he'd reached the other side of the tree he, like Josh, was a boy–eleon. They both had the body of a boy and the head of a tree–dwelling reptile.

'Don't panic,' Petty said. 'I've already got the antidote. It's quick and it stops all this nonsense properly.'

'Wait!' Danny said. His voice sounded odd, coming from his reptilian head—a bit thick and flat.

'Wait?' echoed Josh. 'We're boy–eleons! Freaks of nature! Why wait? Are you looking for a job on *Doctor Who*?'

Danny grinned in a slow, scaly way, and led Josh and Petty along the path that wound into the woods behind the school. 'Just a few more minutes will do it,' he said. 'Petty—can you meet us across the other side?'

'Of course—but why?' asked Petty, clutching the antidote spray.

'Ooooh—I think it's time we started hanging about with Billy and Jason!' Danny said.

A Licky Situation

Billy Sutter and Jason Bilk had a routine. Every day after school they would go to the corner shop to buy sweets with all the money they'd managed to nick from the little kids.

It was a regular thing.

And after they'd bought their sweets they liked to take them into the woods and scoff them in the branches of a big, easy-to-climb oak tree.

Danny and Josh knew this because they also liked to climb the oak tree but had been shoved off it several times by Billy and Jason. Although they fought back, after a while it was just too much aggravation and so they didn't bother with the tree any more. Nor did anyone else from their school. It became Billy and Jason's tree. You could tell by all the plastic wrappers underneath it and the big pink blobs of spat-out bubble gum stuck along its branches.

Today, though, Billy and Jason were going to share.

They crashed noisily through the wood and made straight for 'their' tree. With blazer pockets full of booty they climbed up and got onto a broad branch which was wide enough to sit on comfortably while eating with both hands.

Usefully for Josh and Danny, one of the things which had not faded away since their complete chameleon SWITCH was their agility. Danny had always been good at climbing but now he was brilliant at it. Josh had been average at it—but now he was brilliant too. Five minutes before Billy and Jason had arrived, the brothers had scaled the tree with ease.

As Billy and Jason settled on the wide branch, filling their faces with chocolate and fizz bombs, Danny and Josh hung upside down above them, their legs hooked over a higher branch and their heads visible through the leaves. They were perfectly still. They didn't even blink.

'I got popcorn!' snuffled Jason, pulling a bag
of it out of his other pocket. He opened it up and
the sweet scent rose into the air. 'Shame we didn't
have it for when we was watchin' Josh Phillips on
those ropes. He looked like such a punnet.'

'A punnet?' echoed Billy, opening a bag of
Maltesers. 'What's a punnet?'

'It's a . . . punnet,' mumbled Jason, screwing up
his face.

'What—like you put strawberries in?' snorted
Billy. 'You've gotta work on your insults, Jase.
You're goin' soft in the 'ead!'

'Where'd he go, though?' Jason puzzled. 'After we hoisted 'im up? He just disappeared, like . . . and then came back, 'angin' off the light.'

'Stop tryin' to think, you dunce,' advised Billy. 'You'll have a nosebleed. Gi's some popcorn.'

'Ge'off!' grunted Jason. 'Eat your own stuff.'

'I'll have some,' Josh said, above. And he shot out his tongue and collected seven or eight bits of popcorn on it before pinging it back up into his mouth and munching with enjoyment.

Jason froze and stared into his popcorn bag with confusion. Then he looked up. And stared with more confusion. There was nobody there. Above him all he could see were branches and oak leaves. He turned to stare at Billy. 'Did you just nick my popcorn?' he asked.

'No—*I* did,' Josh said. And he sent his tongue down again and got some more.

'What? Who said that?' Jason jerked his head up and down and from side to side, trying to work out where the voice was coming from.

'And I'll have some of those, please,' Danny said, and sent his tongue down into Billy's bag of Maltesers.

Billy squawked with shock as the stretchy pink thing shot past his face and into his sweets, retreating with about six of them stuck on to it. He nearly fell off the branch as he twisted his head up to see who was there. But he could see nobody. Just branches and leaves.

'Bi—i—ill . . .' Jason said, his voice wobbling. 'What's goin' on?'

'Shattup!' Billy hissed. 'Listen! There's someone up here messin' with us . . . YOU GET DOWN HERE!' he yelled out. 'Get down here and I'll smack your face in!'

'Not very polite, is he?' Josh said to Danny.
'Do you want to go down there and get your face
smacked in?'

'Oddly, no,' Danny said.

'OI! It's the nature nerd and the loser! I know
their voices!' bellowed Jason. 'Get down! Show
yourselves, you maggots!'

'Say please,' Josh said.

Billy said something less polite.

'Oh, all right then,' Danny said. 'We'll show
ourselves.' And then he and Josh moved. That was
all they needed to do. Their heads, poking down
through the leaves, had been in plain sight the
whole time anyway, just camouflaged and perfectly
still.

'Hi, guys!' Josh said, waving.

Danny grinned and let his tongue flop down
again to get some more Maltesers. 'Fanks!' he
mumbled, through a mouthful.

Billy and Jason just *stared* for a few seconds
at the upside down boys with chameleon heads
chortling and shooting long sticky tongues down
towards them.

Then they started screaming and scrabbling to get away.

'Oh don't go NOW!' called out Josh. 'We thought you might like to hang out with us?'

'Aaaaaaaargh! Aliens! Aliens!' squealed Billy.

'It licked me! There's toxic lick on me!' sobbed Jason and fell off the branch, thudding on the leaves and sweet wrappers a couple of metres below with a 'doof' and a whimper. Billy fell down next to him and rolled head–over–heels across the woodland floor, squeaking like one of Piddle's chew toys. They both scrambled to their feet and ran as if they were, indeed, being chased by aliens.

Their screams and howls echoed back through the wood for a couple of minutes and then they were gone. Josh and Danny laughed so hard they almost cried. Except chameleons don't have tear ducts.

Five minutes later they found Petty at the edge of the wood and after two quick blasts of antidote they were normal again.

'I won't even ask,' she said.

Bricking It

'We should tell her,' Josh said, standing up from his microscope, back in their bedroom. He held up the red marble and nodded. 'More code,' he said. 'And a hologram of a cat.'

'You don't think it really could be another kind of SWITCH do you?' asked Danny. He peered at the other coded marble—the blue one—as it nestled in his palm. 'This one's got a sort of bat thing in it—and that's a cat. These are . . . mammals!'

'It does look just like the code in the SWITCH cubes,' said Josh. 'Maybe Petty made it and lost it all, just like she lost the REPTOSWITCH cubes. And maybe the bit of her brain which she says was burnt out by Victor Crouch was *so* burnt out she doesn't remember.'

'But it still doesn't explain why somebody is sending us clues to find them,' Danny said. 'If they want Petty to have them back, why not just send them to *her*?'

As if to answer their question the bedroom door opened and Piddle ran in, looking very excited and important. Once again, someone had tucked something into his collar. A note with some familiar handwriting on it.

'RUN!' yelled Danny. 'They must be right outside!'

But by the time they had reached the front garden there was nobody to be seen in the road at all. 'Piddle! Follow!' Josh said, grabbing Piddle's collar and urging him out onto the pavement. 'Follow whoever gave you that note!' But Piddle just ran around in circles, trying to bite his own tail.

'Forget it,' sighed Danny. 'Let's just read it.'

He opened the note and read:

BRAVO, JOSH + DANNY. I DIDN'T THINK YOU'D GET THIS ONE. SOON . . . No 3! IF YOU DARE . . .

There was no signature, as usual. But Danny did notice something stuck to the corner of the paper. A single black sequin.

'Come on—round to Petty now!' Josh said.

But Petty didn't come when they knocked on the front door, and the new stout side–gate she'd had built was padlocked shut. A light humming told them it was probably electrified on the far side too, so they decided not to climb it.

'Tomorrow,' Josh said, as they walked back up the passage on their side of the fence. 'I don't

think we'll hear any more from Mystery Marble
Sender before then.'

'JOSH! DANNY!' It was their dad, yelling from
the back garden. 'I need you to come and clear out
the garage with me!'

'Oh no,' shuddered Danny. 'I hate garage
clearing. The spiders are *huge!*'

'I'm tired out,' grumbled Josh. 'I want to go and
read my books on my bed.'

Dad's head appeared around the corner of the
house. With a sudden, odd instinct, Josh and
Danny froze against the wall. Then Josh, feeling
guilty, opened his mouth to say 'OK, Dad. Coming.'

But before the words came out he noticed something peculiar. Dad was looking down the side passage . . . but not at them. Keeping perfectly still he swivelled his eyes round to Danny and saw why. He and his brother—and even their clothes—were perfectly camouflaged against the red brick wall.

'Well as soon as I see them, they've got work to do,' Dad said as he stomped right past them and round into the front garden.

'Much more useful side effect than frog's legs,' whispered Danny, and giggling, they crept away to camouflage themselves in the bushes . . .

DIARY ENTRY 657.6

SUBJECT: CREATING A MONSTER

Well it was certainly peculiar to have poor Hector turn into a chamelemouse! Apart from that time when Danny and Josh's legs remained frog-like for a day after their first AMPHISWITCH, this has never happened before. I wonder if REPTOSWITCH is a bit unstable compared to earlier formulas . . .

Still, all's well that ends well and it was certainly nice not to have Josh and Danny yelling at me for nearly getting them killed for a change. They really seemed to enjoy being chameleons . . . and boyeleons!

REMEMBER

My plan to create a second top secret lab—away from spies—is coming on well. It's some distance from here but no sneaky government spook would ever think to look there. And in the meantime I have electrified the side passage and put more laser traps and gas canisters into the main house. Am also planning an emergency incineration system for this lab ... Probably ought to warn Josh and Danny about that.

Also, I get the feeling that there's something they're not telling me. I wonder if they're keeping a little secret? Hmmmmm. May have to use my Patented Potts Secret Detector if they don't come out with it soon ...

YES! The PATENTED POTTS SECRET DETECTOR! BWAHAHAHA! HAHAHAHAAAA!

Aaah. I do like a good evil cackle from time to time. It really clears out the sinuses.

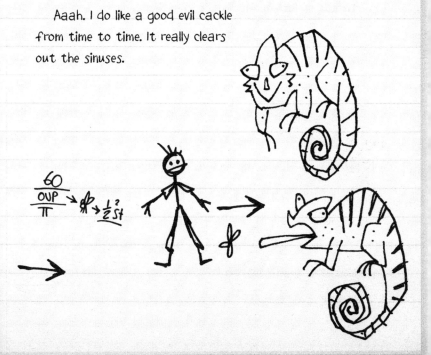

GLOSSARY

Agile—Able to move quickly and easily.

Amphibian—An animal that can live on land and in water.

Antidote—Something which takes away the bad effects of a poison or disease.

Camouflage—A way of hiding things by making them look like part of their surroundings.

Cellular—Made of cells.

Gyrating—Moving around in circles or spirals.

Hijack—To take control of something by force.

Hologram—A type of photograph made by laser beams, that appears to have depth as well as height and width.

Laboratory—A room or building equipped for scientific work.

Mammal—Any animal of which the female gives birth to live young and can feed them with her own milk.

Pincer—The claw of a shellfish such as a lobster. Good for gripping things.

Prehistoric—Belonging to a very long time ago.

Prey—An animal that is hunted by another animal.

Reptile—A cold-blooded animal that creeps or crawls. Lizards and snakes are reptiles.

Scales—The thin overlapping parts on the outside of fish, snakes, and other animals.

Serum—A type of fluid used in science and for medical purposes.

Sphere—A perfectly round solid shape.

Telescopic—To do with telescopes, and seeing things in close detail.

PLACES TO VISIT

Want to brush up on your reptile knowledge? Here's a list of places with special areas dedicated to our scaly friends.

New Forest Reptile Centre
http://www.new-forest-national-park.com/new-forest-reptile-centre.html/

London Zoo
http://www.zsl.org/zsl-london-zoo/

Chester Zoo
http://www.chesterzoo.org/animals/reptiles/

WEBSITES

Find out more about nature and wildlife using the websites below.

http://www.nhm.ac.uk/kids-only/

http://kids.nationalgeographic.com/

http://www.switch-books.co.uk/

http://www.arc-trust.org/

Another exciting adventure awaits . . .

Ali Sparkes

Winner of the Blue Peter
Book of the Year

Illustrated by
Ross Collins

SWITCH

Turtle Terror

A secret potion . . . A world of adventure.

Dangerous Claws

Above the churning sea, a boy clung to the
rocks, the breeze blowing his spiky blond hair
across his face. Above him was glory. Below
him was death. Possibly.

'JOSH!' he yelled to his brother. 'JOSH! Look
at MEEEE!'

A short walk along the beach, Josh was
keeping very still, watching shrimps and tiny
crabs skittering about in a rock pool. Nearby,
Piddle was licking an orange lump stuck to a
rock, his tail wagging wildly. Neither of them
looked up at Danny.

'JOOO-OOOSH!' Danny yelled. 'LOOK!
I'm right up at the top now! I'm like . . .
Spiderman!'

Josh sighed and looked up at his twin. Danny had been scrabbling up and down the rocky Cornish beach all morning. He didn't try to scale the actual cliffs—Mum and Dad had made him promise not to, especially while they were up in the holiday cottage perched on the clifftop above—but the craggy rocks which rose out of the sand were just right for his Spiderman impressions.

'Yeah—great,' Josh yelled back. 'Piddle!' he scolded, as their terrier (named after a certain habit he had when he got excited) flopped his long pink tongue over the orange lump again. 'Leave that poor defenceless anemone alone!' Above the tide the sea creature looked like a half sucked fruit gum, instead of the marigold-like flower it would be under water, but Josh was pretty sure it didn't taste like one. Piddle started digging in the sand instead.

Josh was about to go back to his rock pool gazing when he felt a twinge of nerves and glanced back up again. Danny was very high up this time. The rocky outcrop he had climbed was tall and jutted away from the beach and out into the sea, like a long stony finger. Danny had clambered all the way to the end, where the sea below was lively and deep, and was trying to climb over an awkward ledge and stand up on the top.

But this wasn't what worried Josh. Danny was an excellent climber and it would take a lot to make him to fall. No . . . it was something else. Something which was making its way along the top of the same ledge that Danny was about to get up onto. Something about the size of a rugby ball. Something . . . with eight legs.

Josh jumped to his feet, his heart thumping. He nervously rubbed his sandy hands through his short blond hair and squinted hard at the eight-legged thing. Yep. Even from this distance he was sure what it was . . . and that it was on a collision course.

'DANNY!' Josh yelled, running across the sun-baked sand towards his brother's outcrop. 'DANNY! Come down now! Come down!'

'Why? I'm nearly at the top!' Danny yelled back.

'COME DOWN!' Josh bellowed. The eight-legged thing was just centimetres away from Danny's scrabbling fingers, as he sought a good hand-hold for the final pull up. 'COME DOWN THE WAY YOU WENT UP! DANNY! NOOOOOW!'

But at that point Danny pulled himself up over the ledge and came face to face with one of the things he feared most.

He saw eight legs and a fearsome brown face grimacing at him.

And he screamed.

And fell backwards off the rock.

And hit the sea.

Danny went under like a stone. One second he was scrabbling in the air and the next his world was a blur of roaring, rushing water. Instinct told him to lock up his throat and not try to breathe. At any second a jagged lump of granite could crack open the back of his head or snap his leg. But he was lucky—the area of water he'd fallen into was a churning, whirling cauldron just deep enough. The water broke his fall and stopped him hitting the rocks at the bottom.

Blue-green water, particles of sand, bits of weed and his own hair swirled around him. Danny began to struggle back up to the surface, pulling himself free of the strong undertow tugging at his legs. Ten seconds after he'd fallen in, he burst back onto the surface, gasping desperately for air.

The first thing he saw was a long wooden stick—the end of Josh's shrimping net. Josh was lying flat on his chest on the lower shelf of rock which Danny had first begun his climb from. He was holding the net end and waving the stick at Danny. Piddle was running up and down the rocks, barking furiously. Josh's face was white and his blue eyes round with fear as he shrieked: 'GRAB IT! GRAB IT!'

As the next swell of water pushed him towards the shore, Danny grabbed it.

Soon he was back on the rock shelf next to Josh, spluttering and coughing and blowing gooey

streams of seawater out of his nose while Piddle
happily licked his ear. His knee was bleeding where
it must have scraped against some rock, but apart
from that, he seemed to be OK.

Eventually he turned to Josh and said: 'sp-sp-
spider!'

'*Crab*!' Josh corrected. 'Spider *crab*. Not an
arachnid—a crustacean. Probably migrating right
now, as it's September . . .'

'You—you—you freaky little nature nerd!'
Danny squawked. 'Can't you just SHUT UP for one
minute about your freaky little nature nerdy facts?!
I nearly DIED just then! That spider . . . crab . . .
tried to kill me!'

'Erm . . . no . . .' Josh corrected. 'That spider
crab was just out for a little walk when these huge
flappy hands started whacking at it and a big
ugly human face reared up out of nowhere and
screamed at it. It's probably having a panic attack
of its own now.'

'Oh—that's right! Worry about the spider, why don't you?' Danny muttered. He could never understand how his twin brother could be so different to him. Creepy-crawly stuff just freaked Danny out—but Josh couldn't get enough of it.

'I wonder it there's such a thing as CRUSTASWITCH,' pondered Josh as he sat down next to Danny on their beach mats a few minutes later. Danny was glugging orange squash from a bottle, hoping the sugar in it would help his state of shock, and letting the hot sun dry out his T-shirt and shorts.

'CRUSTASWITCH?' he echoed.

'Yeah—you know,' Josh said, his eyes shining. 'BUGSWITCH turned us into insects and spiders, AMPHISWITCH turned us into frogs and newts and REPTOSWITCH turned us into lizards . . . but imagine being a crustacean! If we were spider crabs we could walk along the seabed. That would be *so* cool. We'll have to ask Petty Potts if she can make a new SWITCH spray!'

'Josh. Pay attention. I am never going to be a spider crab—get that?' Danny said. 'It was bad enough being a spider! And anyway—we're *not* thinking about any SWITCHing, are we? We're just having a holiday—hundreds of miles away from Petty Potts and her secret lab and her SWITCH spray . . .'

'Yeah—I s'pose,' Josh said, lying back on the beach mat and putting his hands behind his head. 'We probably do need a break from all that excitement and danger. Getting turned into insects and spiders and frogs and lizards is amazing—but it wears you out.'

'A nice, peaceful holiday,' agreed Danny. Piddle returned to his hole and carried on digging for a while before heading off up the cliff path, obviously hoping to get some lunch from Mum or Dad at the cottage.

'Yup,' Josh said. 'With *nothing* getting SWITCHed and *no sign* of Petty Potts and her genius experiments anywhere.'

And that was when a parachute landed on the beach next to them.

FUN AND GAMES

There are more games for you to play and
download free on the SWITCH website.

www.switch-books.co.uk

Word search

Search for the hidden words listed below:

DANNY
JOSH
PIDDLE
PETTY
CHAMELEON
SWITCH

SPRAY
EYEBALL
HEADMASTER
ROPES
MARBLE
TONGUE

H	B	Q	T	O	N	G	U	E	Z
P	E	T	T	Y	K	H	S	O	J
G	H	A	I	E	A	W	C	L	R
S	X	C	D	A	N	N	Y	L	O
P	F	M	T	M	G	P	W	A	P
R	K	A	P	I	A	D	H	B	E
A	D	R	C	F	W	S	R	E	S
Y	G	B	H	M	B	S	T	Y	U
B	J	L	P	I	D	D	L	E	A
N	O	E	L	E	M	A	H	C	R

Spot the difference

These pictures *look* the same, but can you spot ten differences?

Answers on page 125

True or false?

Answers on page 125

1. Chameleons are always brown.
2. A chameleon's tongue can be as long as its body.
3. A chameleon's tongue takes one second to shoot out and catch an insect for dinner.
4. Chameleons can look in two different directions at the same time.
5. Chameleons sometimes change colour because of their mood.
6. Chameleons have five legs.
7. 'Chameleon' comes from ancient Greek words meaning 'a lion on the ground'.
8. Chameleons don't have ears.
9. Chameleons have six toes on each foot.
10. Chameleons' upper and lower eyelids are joined.

Jokes

Q) What's the definition of a nervous breakdown?
A) A chameleon on a tartan rug!

Q) What do chameleons have that no other animals have?
A) Baby chameleons!

Q) What is a chameleon's motto?
A) A change is as good as a rest!

Q) Can a chameleon jump higher than a tree?
A) Yes, trees can't jump!

Q) What's a chameleon's favourite game?
A) Hide and seek!

Answers

Word search (page 122)

Spot the difference (page 123)

True or false? (page 124)

1. False—chameleons change colour to blend into their surroundings and hide from predators.

2. True.

3. False—their tongues can shoot out to catch an insect in less than a hundredth of a second.

4. True—their eyes swivel independently of each other.

5. True—oranges and reds suggest a chameleon is excited or annoyed.

6. False—but they do use their tail as a fifth leg—wrapping it around branches for extra stability.

7. True.

8. True—although they may be able to sense vibrations, like snakes.

9. False—they have five on each foot, fused into a group of two and a group of three, giving the foot a tongs-like appearance.

10. True—they see through a pinhole.

About the author

Ali Sparkes grew up in the wilds of the New Forest, raised by sand lizards who taught her the secret language of reptiles and how to lick her own eyes.

At least, that's how Ali remembers it. Her parents, brother and two sisters argue that she grew up in a council house in Southampton, raised by her mum and dad, who taught her the not terribly secret language of English and wished she'd stop chewing her hair.

She once caught a slow worm and it flicked around like a mad thing and she was a bit scared and dropped it.

Ali still lives in Southampton, now with her husband and two teenage sons, and likes to hang out in the nearby Hawthorn Wildlife Centre spying on common lizards. The lizards are considering legal action . . .

Whether you're interested in insects
or revolted by reptiles, you'll love the
SWITCH website!

Find out more about the creatures in
Josh and Danny's adventures, enter fantastic
competitions, read the first chapters
of all of the SWITCH books, and enjoy
lots of games and activities.

www.switch-books.co.uk